Oliver

The Ornament

Meets

Frasier and Merry

Written by Todd M. Zimmermann

Illustrated by Annika Ball

This book is dedicated to children facing difficult times, especially the inspirational children we've met at Children's National Hospital in Washington, D.C. Your bravery, and the bravery of children facing obstacles everywhere, is amazing. We hope that Oliver's message of hope, kindness, and optimism inspires children and families alike; just as these children have inspired us.

Terrianna Starkey

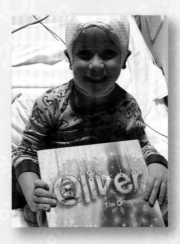

Gabriel Cybulko

Nathan Simm

Riley Whitney

Sofia Martinez

The entire Nelson household was fast asleep. Henry and Holly had gone to bed hours ago, while Mom and Dad had just turned in. Each of the ornaments had also finally fallen asleep after an exciting day. That is, every ornament except for Nellie, the naughty ornament determined to ruin Christmas for everyone.

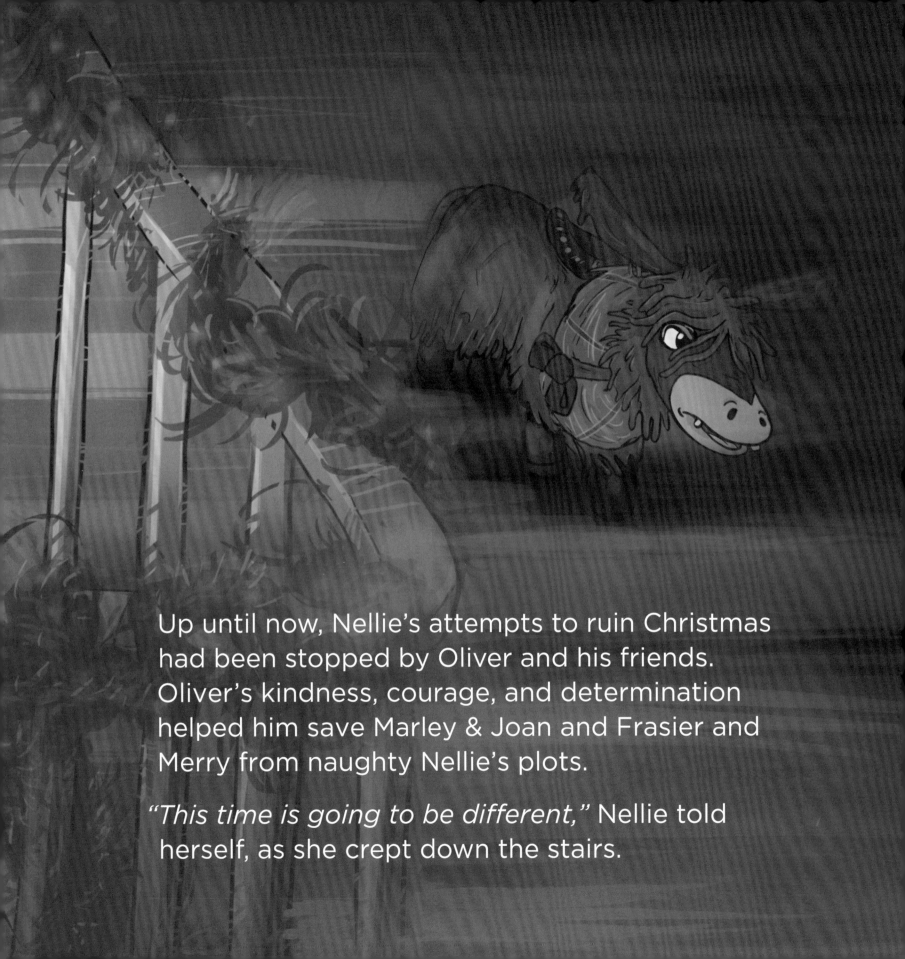

Up until now, Nellie's attempts to ruin Christmas had been stopped by Oliver and his friends. Oliver's kindness, courage, and determination helped him save Marley & Joan and Frasier and Merry from naughty Nellie's plots.

"This time is going to be different," Nellie told herself, as she crept down the stairs.

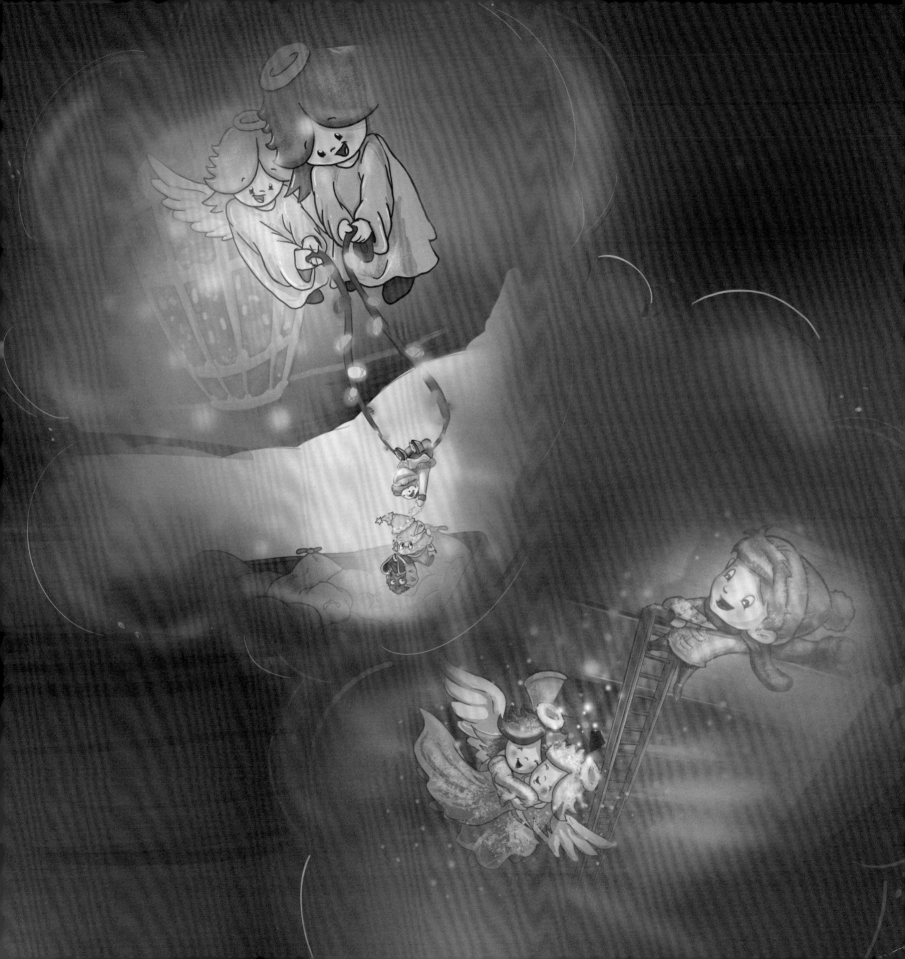

This is the best idea yet," she thought to herself. *"I'm going to get all of them, and teach them a lesson."*

So, Nellie slithered and crawled her way across the floor and went under the Christmas tree. Once at the base, she loosened each of the screws that were holding the tree in place.

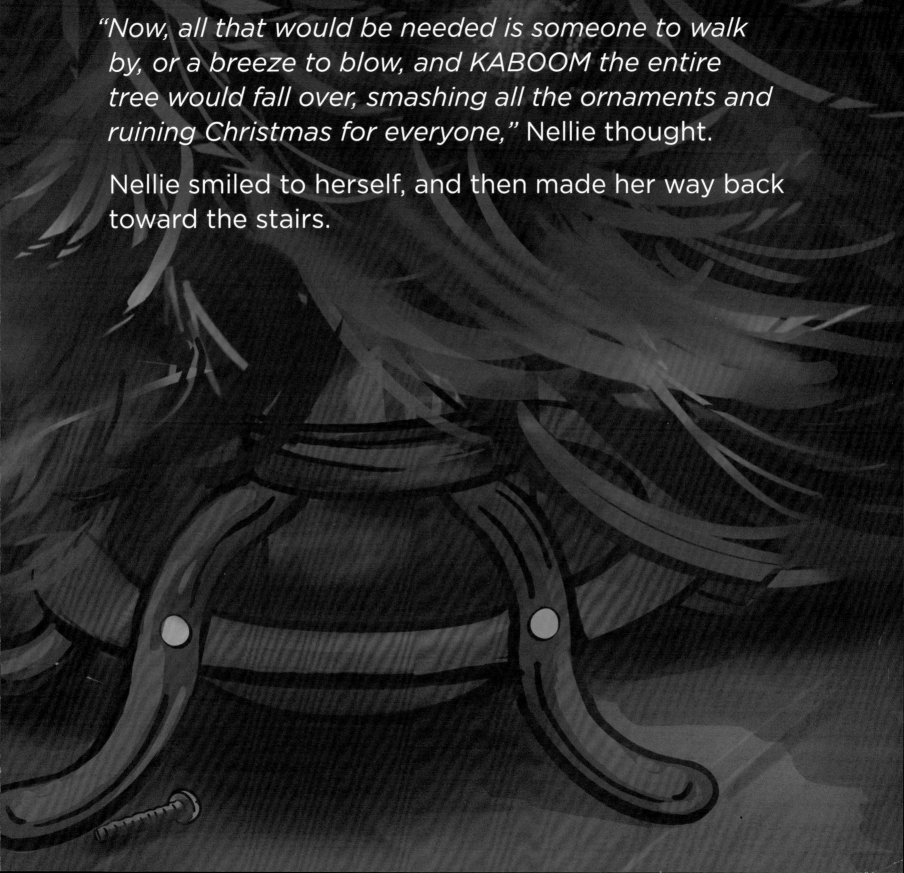

"*Now, all that would be needed is someone to walk by, or a breeze to blow, and KABOOM the entire tree would fall over, smashing all the ornaments and ruining Christmas for everyone,*" Nellie thought.

Nellie smiled to herself, and then made her way back toward the stairs.

"Not so fast," exclaimed Nora to a startled Nellie.

"Let me go," Nellie demanded as Nora's foot was firmly planted on her tail.

"Not until you tell me what you're doing down here," demanded an upset Nora.

"None of your business!" Nellie screamed, as she broke loose and ran back to the attic.

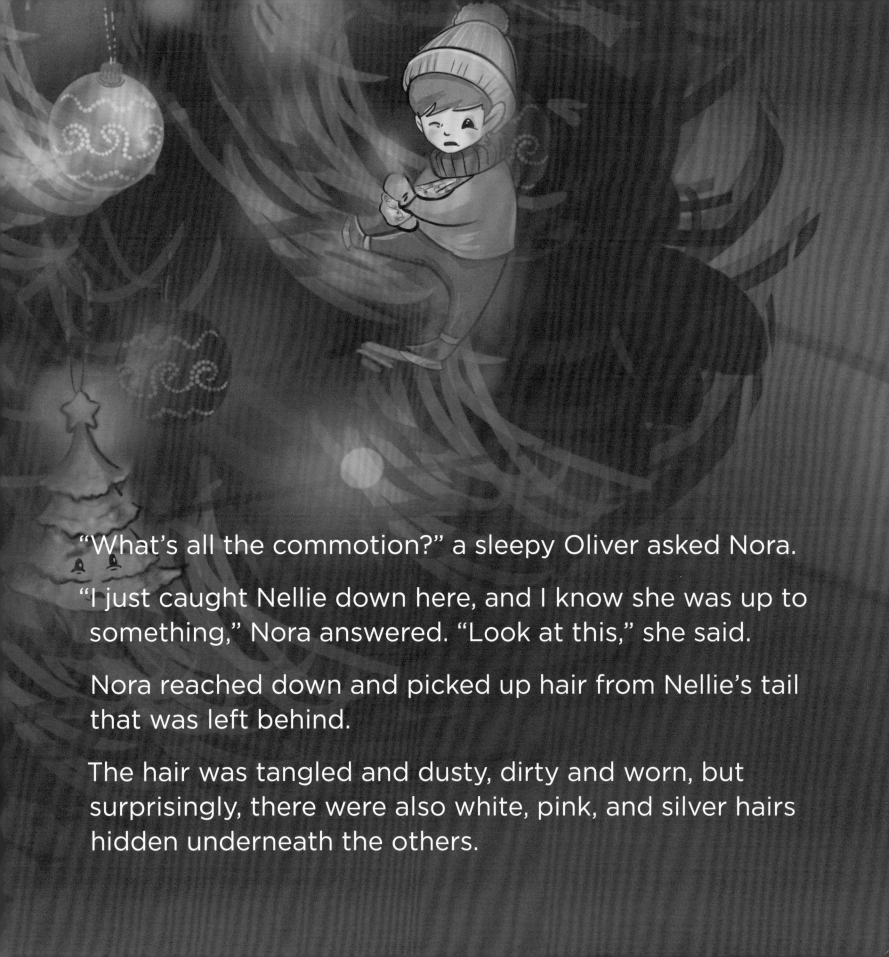

"What's all the commotion?" a sleepy Oliver asked Nora.

"I just caught Nellie down here, and I know she was up to something," Nora answered. "Look at this," she said.

Nora reached down and picked up hair from Nellie's tail that was left behind.

The hair was tangled and dusty, dirty and worn, but surprisingly, there were also white, pink, and silver hairs hidden underneath the others.

By now, all the ornaments had woken, hearing all the commotion. As Nora held the hair from Nellie's tail, Marley & Joan questioned if it was really Nellie that Nora had seen. The hair from the tail simply didn't look like what they had seen when they encountered the angry ornament.

Frasier and Merry agreed, saying, "That looks really cute, nothing like Nellie looks."

After much discussion, but no understanding of what Nellie had done, the ornaments hopped on the tree to go back to sleep. They didn't realize that by doing so, they had tilted the tree a bit, and had loosened it even more.

Then, one by one, each of the ornaments went to sleep.

Rising extra early the next morning, Norb, Teddy, and Nora decided to head to the attic to learn more about Nellie and what, exactly, she was up to.

In the very back corner, they found an old dresser covered in dust and cobwebs. They opened the lowest drawer to find what appeared to be a bed. The bed was made from old newspapers. Really old newspapers. And a picture.

"This has to be a clue," Teddy yelled to Norb and Nora.

"Maybe this will help us understand her better," Nora yelled back to her friends.

"And then we could help her," she finished.

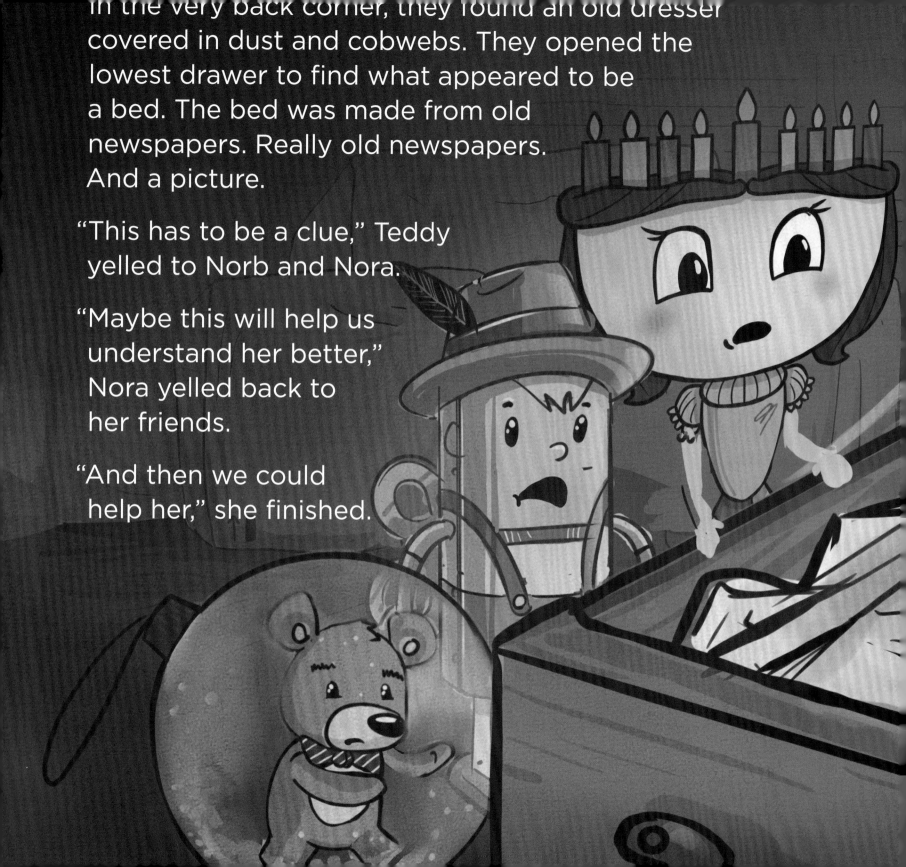

Meanwhile, Nellie was hiding in the other corner of the attic, wondering what the other ornaments were up to.

"Why would they care about me?" she thought to herself.

"This must be another trick. Well, it doesn't matter, before long, the entire tree is going to come crashing down, finishing them all off!"

The three friends went back downstairs to tell the others about what they found in the attic.

"If we understand more about Nellie, maybe we can help her," Oliver told the others. "There has to be a reason why she's so angry."

Listening from the attic, a skeptical Nellie still didn't believe them. *"Why would they want to help me? They're trying to trick me,"* she thought.

Just then, Henry and Holly came to see their friends on the tree.

"Will you tell us another story, Oliver?" asked Henry.

So, Oliver began telling the children about when he met Frasier and Merry.

"Your parents had been married for over a year," Oliver began. "And they wanted to find the perfect Christmas tree and wreath for their new home. They went to store after store, but just couldn't find the right ones."

"The trees that they found were too fat, then too skinny, then too tall, and then too crooked. Hours into the search, your parents began getting frustrated. But, just then, they drove by the most magical Christmas Tree Farm they had ever seen."

"As soon as they walked in, they saw hundreds of the most beautiful Christmas trees ever," Oliver continued.

"How are we going to pick the right one?" Mom asked Dad. "They're all so pretty," she continued.

"After a while, they decided on one in the back corner. A Frasier Fir that they knew was just perfect," Oliver told them.

"Then, they also picked out a wreath for the front door."

"Before leaving, both Mom and Dad snuck into the Tree Farm Gift Shop to buy each other a very special gift," Oliver concluded.

"This is the best tree ever," Dad said to Mom as they began trimming the tree.

"And look how Oliver is right in front," Mom replied.

"Well, I think Oliver needs a friend," Dad said, so he handed Mom a gift box. In it, she found a beautiful Christmas tree ornament. When she opened it, she smiled and said, "We'll call him Frasier."

Oliver continued, "Then, she handed Dad the gift she had purchased for him, saying, *Merry Christmas*. Dad opened it, and saw the beautiful wreath ornament. *Let's call her Merry*, Dad said."

"At that, both Mom and Dad smiled, looking at their new tree, knowing how much joy it would bring to them and their loved ones this Christmas season," Oliver told Henry and Holly.

"You see children," said Oliver, "Every Ornament Tells a Story." Now, Henry and Holly knew how Frasier and Merry got their names, and how nice it is to give gifts to those we love.

Just then, Mom and Dad came in to take Henry and Holly to school.

"That was a great story," said Teddy to Oliver. "I really like…"

Teddy was interrupted by a loud noise coming from the attic. Nellie had started jumping up and down, rattling the entire house. The tree was now waving back and forth as the ornaments all feared for the worst.

"I'm so tired of their stories," she thought to herself, as she continued to pounce on the floor.

"Oh no!" the ornaments all screamed in horror. *"We're going to crash,"* they thought.

Almost as if it were in slow motion, the tree began falling to the ground. Each of the ornaments held on for dear life as the tree stumbled toward the floor.

Just in the nick of time, Oliver jumped off the tree onto the window frame, took off his sling, and lassoed the tree, pulling it back upright to safety.

"So that's what Nellie was doing down here last night," exclaimed Nora. "She loosened the tree."

As Oliver continued to hold the tree, Norb, Belle, and Buck tightened the screws on the stand.

Joan hollered out, "Keep up the good work, Oliver."

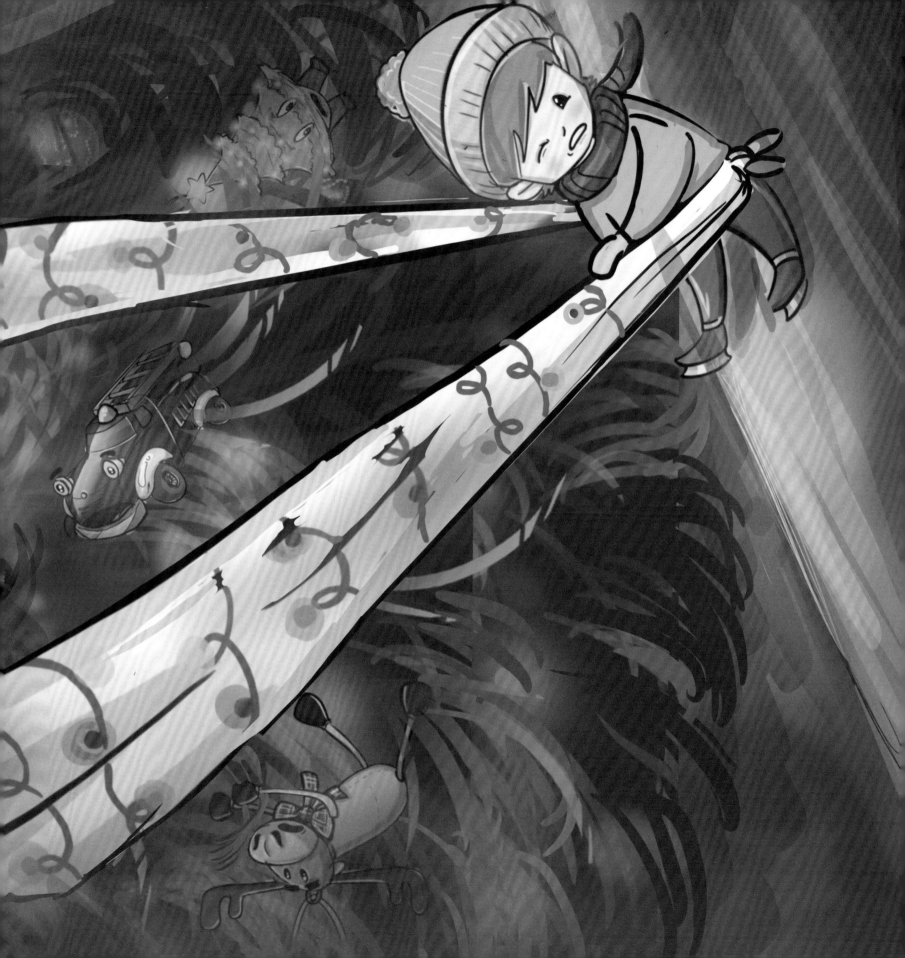

Nellie was watching from the attic in disgust as Oliver once again foiled her plan.

"How could it be that Oliver, the ornament who only had one arm to work with, was always able to save the day? It doesn't make sense," she thought to herself.

Back in the living room, Oliver asked if everyone was alright.

"We're all fine," hollered Norb.

"Everyone looks okay," Buck said.

"Where's Teddy?" asked Merry.

Then, on the other side of the living room, the ornaments all saw Teddy. The shell he was encased in had shattered. "Are you okay, Teddy?" hollered Norb.

"Why are you hollering?" Teddy answered. "I can hear you just fine."

For the first time ever, Teddy didn't have to holler to be heard, and his friends didn't have to holler at him so he could hear.

"I kind of like this," Teddy said, of being out of the shell. "It's kind of fun," he continued, as he began to dance around. "I think I'm going to have to thank Nellie," Teddy joked.

All of the other ornaments laughed and giggled as they watched Teddy dance on the living room floor, enjoying his newfound freedom.

Back in the attic, Nellie was not amused. *"I'll have to find another way to get them,"* she thought.

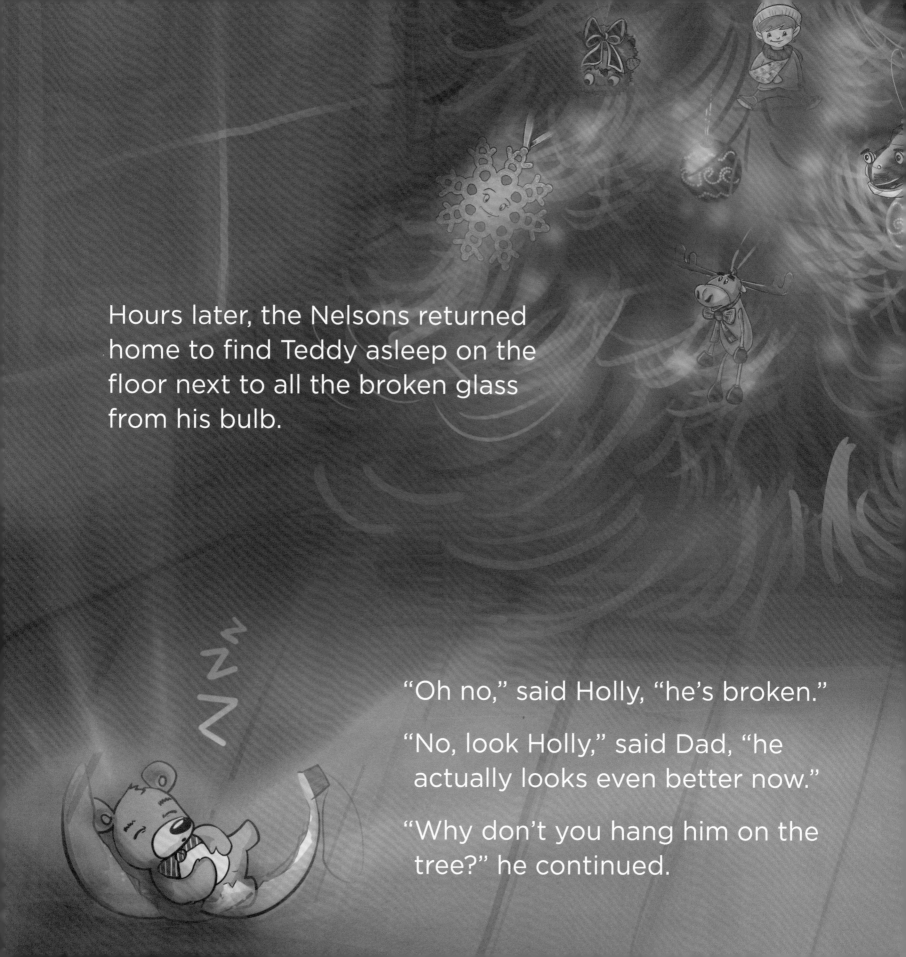

Hours later, the Nelsons returned home to find Teddy asleep on the floor next to all the broken glass from his bulb.

"Oh no," said Holly, "he's broken."

"No, look Holly," said Dad, "he actually looks even better now."

"Why don't you hang him on the tree?" he continued.

So, Dad picked up Holly, who hung Teddy on the tree right next to Oliver. "How did you get Teddy?" Holly asked in a sleepy voice.

"We can tell you that story tomorrow, because Every Ornament Tells a Story," Dad said.

Then, he and Mom took Henry and Holly upstairs and put them to bed.

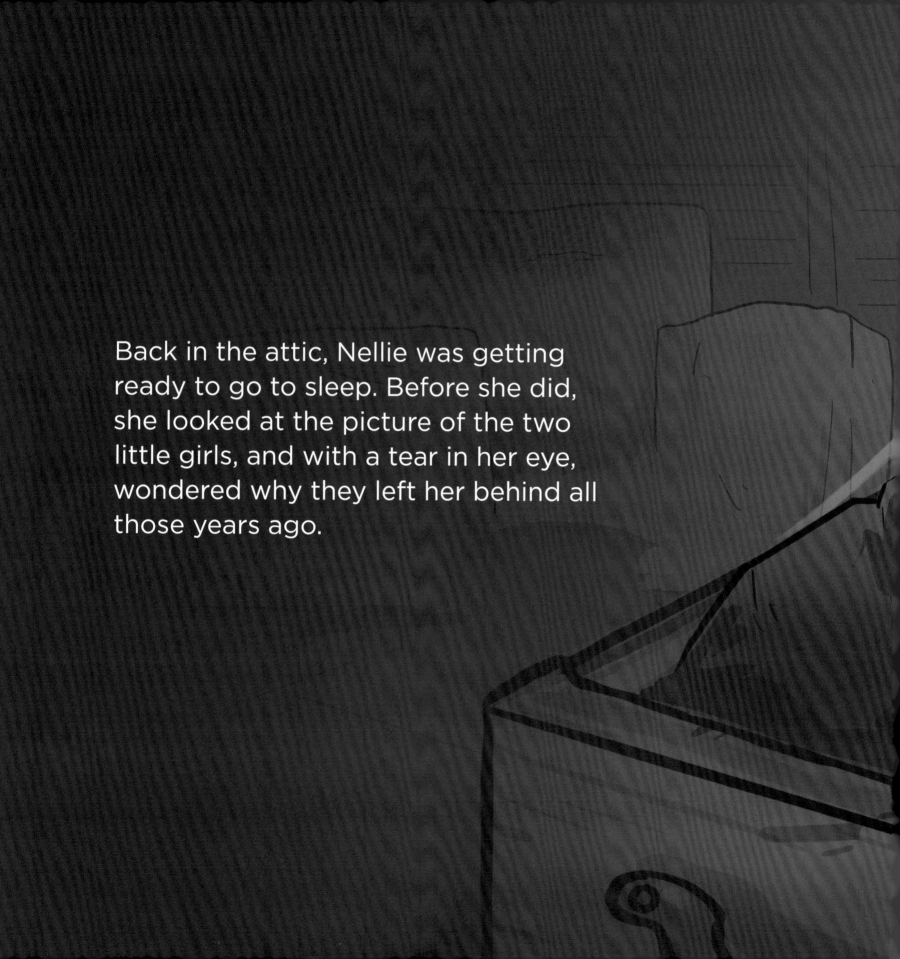

Back in the attic, Nellie was getting ready to go to sleep. Before she did, she looked at the picture of the two little girls, and with a tear in her eye, wondered why they left her behind all those years ago.

After the family went to bed, the ornaments planned their next move to help Nellie. They had a clue, and maybe that could help them understand her better. She had done some really mean things, but it was Christmas, and the ornaments were determined to help her. With those kind thoughts, all the ornaments went to sleep.

And so, dear friends, as you hang us on your tree this year, sit down with your family and have them tell you the stories of all the ornaments on your tree. You never know, there just might be another Oliver, Frasier, and Merry hanging on your own Christmas tree. Because after all, Every Ornament Tells a Story, like the time I met Teddy and Norb . . .

Love,

Oliver

With grateful appreciation to the entire staff of Children's National Hospital in Washington, D.C. for the amazing support you provide to children in need, as well as healthcare workers everywhere. With very special thanks to Annika Ball, Gary Gronlund, Kyle Kostechka, Kyle Meredith, Tom O'Reilly, Adam Soleymani, Erika Q. Stokes, Tom Trucco, and Caryn Weiss.

With the biggest thanks and appreciation reserved for John Hoerst.

In loving memory of our friends and family no longer with us, including: Myron Heffernan, Mary Jane Hemssing, John LaGrassa, Fred Mendell, John Piccolo, Phil Reynolds, Ross Rottmann, Matt Snyder, Bill Sutmar, Doris Zimmermann, and Oliver's biggest cheerleader, Marlene Zimmermann.

Oliver & Friends, Inc.
P.O. Box 13304
Chicago, IL   60613

www.olivertheornament.com

ISBN 978-0-9863416-8-7

Printed in China.

Every Ornament Tells a Story™

Here's A Place For You To Tell Yours

_____

_____

_____

_____

_____

_____

_____

_____

_____

_____

Every Ornament Tells a Story™

Here's A Place For You To Tell Yours

_____

_____

_____

_____

_____

_____

_____

_____

_____

_____

Every Ornament Tells a Story™

Here's A Place For You To Tell Yours

_____

_____

_____

_____

_____

_____

_____

_____

_____

_____

_____